Whiskers an...

Cat stories about c...
and friendship

WHISKERS AND FRIENDS 2

Cat stories about courage, confidence and friendship

WHISKERS AND FRIENDS 2

Cat stories about courage, confidence and friendship

IV. THE TALE ABOUT THE INSECURE JASPER

II. THE GRUMPY CAT AND THE HAPPY CIRCUS

III. THE TALE ABOUT THE BRAVE OLIVER

I. THE TALE ABOUT LUNA AND HER FEAR OF DARK

I. THE TALE ABOUT LUNA AND HER FEAR OF DARK

Once upon a time, in a small town, lived a little cat named Luna. Luna was a beautiful cat with soft, black fur and big, bright eyes. She loved to play and explore, but there was one thing that scared her more than anything else: the dark.

Every night when the sun went down, Luna's heart would start to race. She was afraid of the shadows and the unknown things that could be hiding in the darkness. Luna would hide under her bed and wait until morning, hoping that the night would pass quickly.

One day, Luna's friend, a wise old owl named Oliver, came to visit her. Luna told him about her fear of the dark, and Oliver listened patiently. He told her that sometimes things are not as scary as they seem and that facing her fears would make her stronger.

Luna was hesitant at first, but Oliver encouraged her to take small steps. He suggested that she start by exploring the dark corners of her house during the day when the sun was shining. Luna felt nervous, but she decided to give it a try.

As Luna explored the dark corners of her house during the day, she discovered that there was nothing to be afraid of. She found that the shadows that scared her were just ordinary objects casting their shapes. Luna felt a little more confident and decided to take the next step.

One night, as the sun went down, Luna took a deep breath and left her hiding spot under the bed. She walked slowly and cautiously through the darkness, using her keen sense of smell and hearing to guide her way. Suddenly she heard a noise. The noise cam from outside of the house.

Luna was scared, but she felt she needs to go out and explore. She opened the door and saw a little white kitten in the backyard. The kitten looked miserable and terrified. Suddenly Luna forgot about her own feelings. She bravely went out into the darkness in order to help her new friend.

The little kitten was very young and looked abandoned. Luna took him home and fed him from her own bowl. Only after he was safe and fed, Luna realized that she overcame her own fear. The kitten stayed to live with Luna and they became great friends.

From that day on, Luna was no longer afraid of the dark. She had faced her fears and discovered that sometimes things were not as scary as they seemed and when you need to help someone in danger , your own fears tend to go away. Luna became a brave and adventurous cat, always eager to explore and learn new things. Now it was her turn to help her new friend face his fears.

II. THE GRUMPY CAT AND THE HAPPY CIRCUS

There was a grumpy cat named Whiskers who lived in a small town. Whiskers was known for his sour mood and his tendency to grumble and growl at anyone who tried to approach him. He spent his days sleeping, eating, and generally being grumpy.

One day, Whiskers was walking through town when he heard a commotion coming from the nearby circus. Curious, he decided to investigate.

As he approached the circus tent, he saw all sorts of colorful animals and performers laughing, dancing, and having fun. Whiskers, being the grumpy cat that he was, scoffed at the idea of having fun and thought to himself, "What's the point of all this? It's just a bunch of silly animals and humans doing silly things."

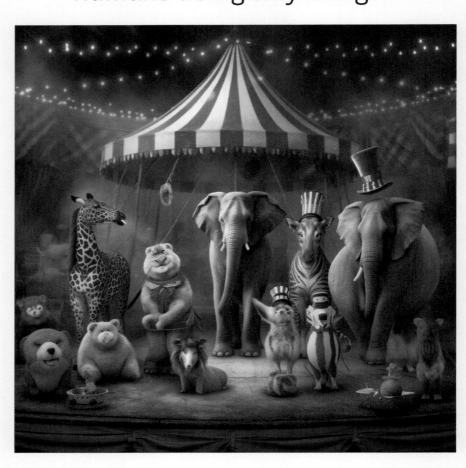

However, as Whiskers watched the performances, he couldn't help but notice that the animals and performers were having a great time. He saw the joy and laughter on their faces and realized that he had forgotten what it was like to have fun and enjoy life.

As the show continued, Whiskers found himself laughing and smiling along with the crowd. He even joined in on a few of the performances, which surprised everyone who knew him as the grumpy cat. Whiskers realized that he had been missing out on the joy and laughter that life had to offer.

After the show, Whiskers went up to the circus owner and thanked him for the performance. The owner smiled and said, "You know, Whiskers, life is too short to be grumpy all the time. Sometimes, it's important to let loose and have some fun."

Whiskers took the owner's words to heart and decided to try and be less grumpy from that day forward. He began to appreciate the small moments of joy and laughter that life had to offer, whether it was chasing a butterfly or snuggling up with his owner.

Whiskers' newfound appreciation for laughter and fun even spread to the other animals and humans in the town. He began to participate in community events and showed a newfound enthusiasm for life.

The grumpy cat had become a happy cat, and everyone in the town noticed the change. They appreciated Whiskers' newfound positive attitude and welcomed him into their lives with open arms.

And so, Whiskers continued to live his life with a newfound appreciation for laughter and fun. He still had his grumpy moments, but he knew that life was too short to waste on negativity. He chose to focus on the good in life and spread joy and laughter wherever he went.

III. THE TALE ABOUT THE BRAVE OLIVER

Oliver was a magnificent cat that lived long ago in Whiskerville, a sleepy little hamlet. Oliver was not your typical cat. He stood out from the others due to his fiery temperament and strong sense of justice. Oliver wandered the streets, always on the alert for any indication of injustice, while other cats lazed around in the sun.

Oliver came into a disturbance near the neighborhood park one sunny afternoon as he was patrolling the area. Smaller cats were being bullied by a pack of intimidating dogs that were growling and barking menacingly at them. The cats huddled together in dread, their eyes wide with terror.

Oliver saw the unfair treatment and his heart blazed with rage. He was aware that he had to speak out against this injustice and save the defenseless kitties. Oliver launched himself into action with a resounding meow that cut through the commotion.

Oliver puffed up his hair, raised his tail, and extended his claws as he bounded toward the dogs with unrelenting intent. The daring cat who ventured to approach the dogs caused the dogs to suddenly freeze. Oliver, though, had unwavering courage and kept his stance. Say, "Leave these cats alone!" Oliver commanded power with his voice as he glared at the confused hounds. I won't allow you to ruin the calm and serenity in this community. The dogs looked at each other, unsure of how to respond to this bold cat. They were taken aback by Oliver's fearlessness, and for a brief second, their intimidating façade broke down. Oliver grasped the chance to reason with them since he felt they were vulnerable.

Oliver said, his voice softened but firm, "You don't have to be bullies." "We can all live in harmony while being nice and compassionate. The appropriate course can be chosen at any time. The dogs thought over Oliver's remarks, and a glint of comprehension appeared in their eyes. They slowly receded into the distance, their tails tucked between their legs.

As word of Oliver's heroics spread across Whiskerville, the community celebrated him as a champion of justice and bravery. He gained popularity, and cats from various backgrounds looked to him for protection and instruction. The cats of Whiskerville began to unite and form a close-knit society where they spoke up against injustice after being inspired by Oliver's indomitable attitude. They coordinated nonviolent demonstrations against animal abuse, came together to defend the town's wildlife, and pushed for the fair treatment of all living things.

Oliver's influence extended beyond Whiskerville's boundaries. As word of his exploits spread, cats in nearby towns were moved to action against injustice. They came to understand that regardless of their size or species, they too could contribute.

As the years went by, Whiskerville transformed into a symbol of justice and heroism owing to the valiant deeds of one exceptional cat. Oliver left a lasting legacy, showing all cats that they have the ability to fight injustice and build a better world.

IV. THE TALE ABOUT THE INSECURE JASPER

A cat by the name of Jasper used to reside in the thriving city of Meowville. Unlike his brilliant and self-assured feline friends, Jasper struggled with insecurity. He was persuaded that he lacked any unique abilities or characteristics that made him stand out from other cats, and so felt inferior to them.

Jasper enjoyed watching the other cats as they expertly climbed trees, caught mice with ease, and gracefully leaped through the air. He felt inferior to them and compared himself to them. I'm not as intelligent as Whiskers, he thought. "Max is stronger than I am. I'm not as attractive as Luna is."

Jasper's self-doubt increased and hung over everything he did. He stayed away from people out of concern for his peers' opinions. He merely stayed within the confines of his comfort zone since he thought that anything he tried would fail.

Jasper was sitting alone in the park one dismal afternoon when Sage, an experienced senior tabby cat, came up. Sage knelt down next to Jasper and said, "Dear Jasper, I've been watching you for quite some time. Do you realize that you, like every cat, have certain abilities and qualities? Jasper looked up, his eyes filled with uncertainty.

"But what can I possibly be good at? I'm not as impressive as the other cats."

Jasper, it's true that you might not have the same talents as Whiskers, Max, or Luna, but it doesn't mean you aren't talented, Sage said with a kind smile. Every cat has unique strengths that are just waiting to be found.

Sage added, "You may not be the fastest climber or the toughest hunter, but have you ever noticed how you cheer others up when they're feeling down? Jasper's interest peaked, he listened carefully. You have a talent for empathizing with others and making them feel appreciated and cherished.
As Jasper considered Sage's comments, his eyes became wider. He had never thought of his capacity to console others as a useful talent. Jasper was inspired by Sage's observation and made the decision to investigate this fresh viewpoint.
He began going to the neighborhood shelter, where he spent time with lonely and abandoned cats, giving them comfort. The cats at the shelter started to find comfort in his presence.

as he developed a natural aptitude for calming frayed hearts

As word of Jasper's sympathetic personality spread across Meowville, both cats and people began to seek out his services. His visits to clinics, nursing homes, and schools made people feel better and made them smile.

Jasper gained more self-assurance and became more aware of the special skills he possessed. He stopped evaluating himself in relation to others after recognizing that his genuine worth was not determined by the same standard.

Jasper's ability to empathize quickly became apparent to the cats of Meowville, who praised him for his exceptional skill. They honored his services to the neighborhood and acknowledged that his capacity for solace and joy was just as significant as his brains or physical skill.

Jasper's path of self-discovery taught the city of Meowville an essential lesson: everyone carries something truly remarkable within them, regardless of how uneasy or uncertain they may feel.

From that moment on, Jasper's tale served as a warning to all cats—and even to humans—that measuring our value against that of others is unjust. Instead, it resides in accepting and developing the special talents each of us possesses and using them to improve the lives of people around us.

The

End!

Printed in Great Britain
by Amazon

34434379R00032